D1456644

TO THE RIM OF THE MAP

Veritas Press
1250 Belle Meade Drive
Lancaster, PA 17601

First edition

TO THE RIM
OF THE MAP

STORY BY ERIC VANDERHOOF
PAINTINGS BY LOUISE BREWER

Veritas Press

THIS BOOK IS DEDICATED TO

My loving wife Lisa,
who is called 'blessed'
by her children.
—E.V.

My Dad.
—L.B.

Tim and Deb sat on a big rig.
They did all fit, but they were rib to rib.

The pig and the ram
were in the dim pen.

Dad sat with ten men to gab
and rap at the map.

The big rig ran with pep.
It did dip, but it did not tip.

The big rig was a fit rig.

Tim and Deb were not mad. Tim and Deb were fed a bit of fin that was in the net.

They did get a sip
at the bag.

Dad fed the pig and the ram
in the bin at the pen.

The big rig sat and
it ran not a bit.

The men were in a fit.
Were they to get rid of the map?

No! The map was not bad.
Tim and Deb were sad.

Tim and Deb did beg
to get a bed.

They were to get a nap.

The pig and the ram
were not big and fat.

They were not fed a tid bit.

Dad and the men met to beg a bit with God.
The big rig ran a tad bit.

The big rig ran with the map.

Tim and Deb were set in the bed.

Tim and Deb ran to the
tip of the big rig.

What was that rim
that sat as a dam?

26

Dad and the men did tap at the map.
The map did not fib!

The big rig ran with pep
to the rim of the map.

The pig and the ram were to get fed.
They were set to get fit and fat.

Tim and Deb ran and met Dad.
They all sat at the tip of the big rig

and met with God.